Bubbles and Billy Sandwalker

Written by

Cyndie Lepori

Illustrated by

Layne Keeton Murrish

Copyright© 2012 by
Cyndie Lepori

Material in this book may only be reproduced or transmitted in whole or in part in any medium (whether electronic, mechanical or otherwise) with written permission of Cyndie Lepori

ISBN: 978-0-9856754-1-7

Library of Congress Control Number: 2013932234

DolphinHugs4u2, Stringer, MS

DEDICATION

I dedicate this book to the dolphins and all the beings on and off the planet that are teaching humanity a better way to be, and most humbly teaching me every day and transforming my life so that I can share these joyful life changing lessons with others. For this, I am grateful.

Acknowledgments

I would like to acknowledge my dolphin guides and angels who showed me this book in dream time long before I wrote it; Layne Murrish, my illustrator, who tirelessly painted my visions; and Debbie Reinertson, who was instrumental in getting it edited.

I would like to acknowledge my son, Charlie Ainsworth, who taught me what little boys are made of - LOVE.

I thank the dolphins, sea beings, angels, guides and masters, who were my inspiration and source of much knowledge. And of course, I must thank the pupples who taught me animal communication and continue to patiently teach me not only unconditional love every day but also the value of laughter.

Although there are many truths and experiences that I have lived and from which I have taken my inspiration, please know this is a work of fiction; any resemblance to any person living or dead are purely coincidental.

Table of Contents

Chapter 1	Sea Aquarium	Page 1
Chapter 2	Meeting Seasea	Page 6
Chapter 3	The Sailboat Trip	Page 12
Chapter 4	Bubbles the Dolphin	Page 15
Chapter 5	The Magic Cottage	Page 23
Chapter 6	The Pupples Speak	Page 32
Chapter 7	Bubbles in Dreamtime	Page 38
Chapter 8	Friends of the Sea	Page 45
Chapter 9	The Healing Chamber	Page 49
Chapter 10	Bubble School	Page 53
Chapter 11	Healing of the Golden Rays	Page 65
Chapter 12	Billy and Sandy	Page 71
Chapter 13	Earth's Future	Page 79

Orca Rules

Observe

Respond, Respectfully,

Compassionately

Always

Chapter 1

Sea Aquarium

As Billy Sandwalker walked and looked at the crystal blue waves from the beach, one day he came upon a beautiful dolphin swimming along beside him in the water about 100 yards from shore. She was with a pod of several other dolphins, and the funny thing he noticed as he picked up shells and other interesting and beautiful treasures for his beach collection box was that they seemed to follow him where ever he went on the beach.

It was just after lunch when his mom said he could hit the beach and play. Every day he lived to go to the beach! Mornings were spent going with his mom shopping (which was not his favorite thing to do) and doing "chores". He was out of school for the summer and living in Navarre, FL in a small cottage on the beach. There were just the three of them. He had no brothers or sisters. At times it was lonely, but most of the time it was great!

Billy really loved dolphins and had gone to several sea aquariums to see them up close. He always had a good time and felt a real connection with them. The trainers said they were mammals and were very smart. Even though he loved the dolphins, when he was there he was very sad for them. He did not understand why they were in a tank that seemed much too small and not as free as the dolphins he always saw in a distance from the shore. They did not feel the same. Billy felt there was something much, much more about the dolphins, but he just could not figure out what.

You see, he was a very special boy with big blue eyes just like the sea and sandy colored hair just like the beach. He had always been able to see things that others did not seem to see, and that made him feel very odd and uncomfortable. Well, he had always had the ability to tell when someone was not telling the truth or was sending out information that was not exactly correct, even when they thought it was. Just as the sour note on the piano doesn't feel right or true, what he saw in people made him feel the same way. He also knew things about people, too. And many of these things that he knew about people, according to his parents, there was no way for him to know.

Most of the time he stayed alone thinking and questioning everything, and his parents really did not know what to do about that. He was much more comfortable in the water and on the beach than in the house. TV held no interest for him unless it was a program about the ocean or ocean beings. His parents wanted him to have lots of friends, watch TV, play video games, and just be normal. For him, the TV was just too noisy and bright, the video games were silly or too flashy and violent, and he just did not know how to be normal.

As they swam gracefully in the water he could clearly see energy around the dolphins. The color was unmistakable; it was beautiful crystal neon blue. When the dolphins did not feel good, he knew it right away because their energy would change from this beautiful crystal blue to sickly yellow green. No one seemed to talk of this, but he had seen it several times. When he asked about it, and not knowing that others didn't see this, they always showed a funny look on their faces and either changed the subject or told him that there were no colors around the dolphins. He could also see these colors around people. His mom and dad said they didn't exist, but he knew. To Billy, everyone looked like a rainbow, and the colors changed from person to person.

Billy knew and really liked the trainers, but felt that they sometimes were mistaken about the true nature of the dolphins and other animals of the sea. He really wanted to know more and what was true of them, so he was a regular visitor. And being very curious, he read all he could find about the beings of the sea from mermaids to dolphins. He wanted to work at the sea aquariums when he grew up and make life better for the dolphins living there.

One day, when his parents pulled into the parking lot at the sea aquarium, he could feel the excitement of the dolphins. It was as if they knew he was there. A part of him felt like he was making it up and a part of him really knew he was right. When his parents delayed in the parking lot for a long time, the energy seemed to shift and it felt like they were miffed! He hurried into the building and instead of lingering at the different fish tanks at the entrance, he ran to the dolphins' tank windows.

Normally they seemed to greet him, but this time, he couldn't seem to find them at all. At every window they moved until they were out of his sight. He wanted so badly to see them! After looking in every window and feeling a bit confused, he gave up and was staring at a poster on the wall. Suddenly, his mom yelled out "Look here, Billy!!" When he turned around, all three dolphins were at the window looking directly at him as if to say, "Where did you go?" He laughed so hard he rolled on the floor! He realized that the more he wanted from the dolphins, the more they did not show up and avoided him. What a great lesson!

Being a very smart nine year old, Billy questioned everything and would try different things, too. Since he could see the colors around the dolphins and see when they were happy, sad or sick, he started to feel little pings on his skin as the dolphins noticed him and came to check him out. The trainers told him that the dolphins had sonar and that they could even see inside of him, just like the x-ray that he had when he had fallen and hurt his arm.

One day when he was there, he noticed that one of the dolphins named Lilly was paying particular attention to a thin woman who was standing at the side of the tank. Lilly spent a long time sending colors at a dark area the woman had in her abdomen. The interaction was fascinating and Billy watched in awe. She giggled and spoke to the dolphin. It lasted an abnormally long time and when she took off her hat Billy saw she had no hair. She was very pale and did not look healthy. He wandered close enough to hear her conversation with her family. "I thought I was too sick to come," she said with a giggle. "The last round of cancer medicine made me feel weak and sick, but I feel great now."

He already knew that when people had things wrong, the energy around them changed. Often, he would see the dolphins go to them and send out bubbles that changed their colors. He continued to watch the lady's bubble of energy turn from a dull gray to a beautiful green. And when Lilly swam away, the woman's bubble was a pretty pink and yellow. Her skin turned from pale and gray to pretty and pink.

The dolphins had sent little energy colored bubbles that bounced from the dolphins to him and back. It always made him feel better to know that the dolphins knew him inside and out and they sometimes shared colors. He loved the pink love that came from his heart and theirs.

One day, it came to him that perhaps he could share colors with the dolphins. Standing at the window, he sent pink love from his heart to the dolphins. Suddenly, every dolphin in the tank was looking at him through the window. It made him very happy to give to them too. It seemed that the dolphins gave a lot to people. Dolphins are very patient, and Billy could see how they were patient with the trainers. They seemed to understand the trainers. Although the trainers loved the dolphins, they didn't understand them or know who the dolphins really were, just as Billy's parents did not really know who he was. Billy smiled when he realized that he and the dolphins had this in common.

When the trainers arrived, and it was time to "put on a show" for the visitors, the dolphins splashed and blew bubbles of colors at the trainers to shift their energies up and make them smarter and happier. He always saw the beautiful clear yellow that he had come to know as "joy" that the dolphins sent to the crowds and came back to them. It was a beautiful thing to see.

He truly wondered about all this and knew there was a lot to learn about dolphins, but he just didn't know who to ask who wouldn't think he was crazy, or call him that odd little boy. He decided that he would wait and see. Wise beyond his years, he knew that the answer would reveal itself. Sooner or later, it always does.

Chapter 2
Meeting Seasea

All these thoughts were running through his mind the next day at the beach. He could feel the crystal sand squeaking and squeezing between his toes, the warmth of the sun rays hitting his shoulders, and the salty fishy smell of the Gulf of Mexico. There was very little wind so the waves rolling in were very small and gentle. It was just the kind of day that his parents would let him loose on the beach and he could swim all he wanted as long as he did not go too far out. He had always been more comfortable in the water than on land, and everyone said that he "swam like a fish". He couldn't remember not being able to swim or not loving the water or the beach. Dad called him his "little merman".

Fully present in his body and on high alert, Billy watched the dolphin pod carefully. There were many differences between the wild dolphins and the tame dolphins that he had seen in the sea aquariums. The energy of the wild dolphins seemed much larger and wider. When he could get close enough, he could see the colors wrapping all around him and them and streaming all through the waters around them. He could not even see the edges of the colors. They seemed to linger for hours after the dolphins swam, leaped and played merrily down the Gulf waters. The very nature and feel of the water was changed by the dolphins and whales. If it was murky and dark, it felt light and silvery and brighter after the dolphins and whales came through. He thought it was an amazing insight and felt it would be wonderful to share it with others! But he was just a kid, and the adults didn't have any idea what he was trying to describe, let alone have any interest. Billy felt it was just one more thing that made him odd and different.

One time, his parents took him to a doctor who told them that he was slightly autistic and tried to put him on medications. The medications made him sleepy and unable to see the energies. He started spitting them out and simply refused to take them. At that point, the doctor said he did not think that the medications were helping anyway and reassured his parents that he would grow out of it. He certainly hoped not! He loved his ability to see things that other people could not!

Billy remembered one time when his Mom and Dad had taken him to a strange festival. They said it was for the "Woo-Woos". He saw a woman sitting at her booth blowing bubbles. She looked at him very strangely and told his parents that he was an Indigo Star Child. She told him he was a very special soul and that he had come to this planet to help with the waters. He had a special mission in being born on this planet at this time and he would soon know and understand what it was. She seemed to know him inside and out. When he looked into her eyes, he realized with a start that she really did see him for the special child that he was. Her name was Seasea and she told him in no uncertain terms that the colors he saw were real, and not to allow anyone to tell him differently. This woman who called herself the "dolphin woman" had the same color around her as the dolphins, and when he looked into her eyes, it was like a dolphin gazing back at him. It was strangely comforting! He remembered her often, and it brought him comfort because finally one adult understood him.

SeaSea also told him a lot more and he wished that he could remember it all, but she reassured him that he would remember what she said as he needed to. He had kept the bottle of bubbles she gave him in his treasure chest, and when he blew a bubble, it brought him instant joy, and he smiled with great pleasure. It was like keeping a bottle of happiness. "Remember the bubbles," she said. "There is wisdom in the bubbles that will be shown to you." The information rang true and clear as he watched her heart. She was one of the few adults he had met who seemed to have some of the talents that he had. The strangest thing is that in 5 minutes she seemed to know him and he seemed to know her better than some people he had known all his life. He often wondered about that. It was true magic. He often saw her and spoke to her in his dreams. He knew it was real! At times his dreams were more real than when he was awake! It certainly seemed so anyway. Then again, he traveled to many wonderful places in his dreams.

All of this instantly raced through his mind as he watched the bottle nose dolphins gradually come closer and closer. The dolphins swam in their own way, lazily going up and down like a roller coaster. He never mistook them for sharks because he had seen sharks in the water before, and they swam in a very straight line. Nothing like the dolphins!

Other times, he would sit on the beach and watch the dolphins play games with people. Adults would want to swim with them and they would disappear just as the adults reached them and appear just as the adults came out of the water. It was as if the dolphins enjoyed these games. Their energy certainly turned yellow and gold with joy when he watched this. When he saw the dolphins from the beach, they would swim behind people within touching distance and people did not seem to see them, even when the dolphins were within reaching distance. The dolphins were masters at hide and seek. They also would jump out of the water for certain people, and he had even seen them seem to disappear in mid air.

He remembered that one time when he was in the water, they had allowed him to reach for a fin and towed him back to shore in front of everyone! They then disappeared for the day. It was as if the Mama dolphin had decided that he was too far out and needed to be rescued. As a matter of fact, he had been out a little too far and he was getting very tired. He had read about people being rescued who were in trouble at sea and had not really believed it until it happened to him.

The trainers at the sea aquarium had been very opinionated about swimming with the dolphins. They said that if there were dolphins in the water, be sure and leave the water because they were wild and could be very aggressive. He had read everything that he could find on dolphin behavior and knew that if the dolphins did not want to interact with people, they simply left. They were much better swimmers than the fastest people on the planet. When he looked at the trainers' hearts, he saw that they were trying to be loving and protective of the wild dolphins, but he just did not feel that scaring people about the dolphins was the way to go about it. In his reading he learned that humans were much more dangerous to the dolphins than the dolphins were to the humans!

Chapter 3

The Sailboat Trip

Billy and his parents were headed to Destiny, FL to go on a beautiful sailboat and see the dolphins. This was the highlight of his life. As he walked on the pier he heard a boat captain talking about the latest game that the dolphins were playing. He had a really big boat with lots of fishing poles. When he was out on the water, and there were people fishing, just as they got their fish reeled in close to the boat, the dolphins would race in and snatch the red snapper right off the hooks! Billy really thought the dolphins were very smart in learning how to avoid the hooks, but he also thought it was a very dangerous game. He could see and hear the red anger and frustration of this gruffy old boat captain.

It was then he realized that not everyone loved dolphins and not everyone wished them well. It worried and disturbed him, and in that moment, he understood the need to protect the dolphins from people. A very startling revelation! Seeing that half the boats in the harbor were fishing boats, and the other half were for dolphin cruises, he made up his mind to be protective of the dolphins since he loved them so much. Billy had read that the dolphins were protected under the law of the United States, but who really knows what happens when there was no one around to see?

On board the Dolphin Cruise when they lifted the sail, it was quite a ride! It was quiet. The dolphins came around in droves. It was the most dolphins in one spot that Captain Lora had ever seen. They looked him in the eye as they played in the waves that the sailboat created. There was definitely a magic energy passing between them and him! Everyone on the boat was commenting about it. Billy realized that the Dolphin Woman he had met at the festival was also on the cruise! He was so glad to see her as she stood right beside him and laughed and played! Billy noticed that Captain Lora and Seasea (the Dolphin Woman) knew each other well. He saw that their energy was the same.

There were dolphins in the water and dolphin people on the boat. Their energy was the same. WOW was Billy's reaction! He was truly excited! The very air and water was charged with colors and beautiful energy every where they went, and the dolphins were delighted to see them as much as they were delighted to see the dolphins! Seasea looked at Billy and said, "The dolphins have much to teach us, and you will have wonderful adventures with them. When you pay attention to the dolphins, Billy, they will have gifts for you!"

Even though Captain Lora had said when they cast off that there was no guarantee that they would even see dolphins, everyone on board was gleefully excited when many, many pods came to visit the boat.

"Of course," said Seasea, "this is our true family!" Billy wondered what she meant when she said that. She was very mysterious and cryptic! Billy knew he carried the True Dolphin Heart when she told him his true learning from the dolphins would come in time; a time when the dolphins were ready and he was, too! Billy couldn't wait, but he knew he had to.

Captain Lora made it very clear that it was against the law to feed the dolphins anything. It was bad, too, because it teaches them to depend on humans for food, and to compete for fish with each other. She said this translates into aggressive behavior. How sad it was for Billy to realize how dangerous the humans are to the dolphins. It suddenly occurred to him that people need to learn from the dolphins, NOT the other way around! When the boat returned to the harbor, Billy was full of wonder and delight and, as usual, had many questions running around in his head.

Chapter 4

Bubbles the Dolphin

After a few days of clouds and rain, the sun returned, and Billy was itching to go down to the beach. When he finally got there, he sat on the sugar white sand and was closely watching a whole dolphin pod when, suddenly, they came nearer to shore. They had found a school of fish and were tossing the fish around before eating them. He had seen this before and thought it must be a very fun dolphin game!

At first there were only two or three, and then more and more gathered until he counted 15 or 20. It was so amazing to watch them swimming side by side and touching only when they wanted to! They were swimming through the waves and leaping for joy, from the baby dolphins to the older ones! It was amazing that they never ran into each other! Billy admired their power and agility!

He wanted to be a dolphin! He had dreamed of being a dolphin! He had never been comfortable with being a human. He could resist no longer, and slowly went into the cool blue beautiful water. He was so glad that he had brought his mask, snorkel and fins. He could see as clearly under the water with his mask on as he could on land. And he could see very well in the clear blue water where it was shallow even with his mask off.

He did not swim toward the dolphins, but swam slowly about 100 yards away from them to wait and see what would happen. He was very respectful that way. He could hear their chatter and squeaks as they communicated with each other. It was as if he had entered another world. He was weightless and free! The water was the perfect temperature! As he swam out, the water at times got hot and cold. His dad called these thermoclines. That meant that there were "rivers" of water at different temperatures that flowed through the water. It was hard to understand how there could be rivers in the water, but he knew it was true just from experience.

There were a million tiny fish swimming all around him. He could see shells, sand dollars and other sea life on the bottom. The tiny fish were orange and white and seemed to surround him in magic! They nipped at his skin, and he loved to watch them swim all around. He could hear the sounds and clicks they made to each other. Beneath him, he spotted the golden stingrays. He even spotted a small sea turtle gliding by that seemed to fly through the water as it swam round and round him. He laughed in delight at the underwater antics of these beautiful beings and their unique gifts that they seemed to be giving him. You would think that the water would be very silent, but in truth it was amazingly noisy.

It was so much fun that for a moment he forgot all about the dolphins, besides listening to the beautiful tones being sent by them through the waters. One of the dolphins came by with a leaf draped over her fin. She dropped it right in front of Billy. Billy looked at the leaf in wonder as the dolphin snatched it away just as he reached for it. This happened several times as Billy flooded his mask laughing. The dolphin was teaching him the leaf game. It was playing with him. It was definitely going to be an unusual afternoon.

She was an older bottle nose dolphin that looked very wise. She swam very slowly and carefully by. She was much, much bigger than he was. Her skin was gray and looked rubbery, yet she had very captivating eyes. There were marks on her beautiful gray skin that said she had perhaps had a few not so friendly encounters in the sea. He could not tell if it was boat propeller scars or from the sharks that he knew roamed the waters. It really did not matter, except it would help him to get to know her and recognize her in the future.

When a dolphin wants to be your friend, it will come by and look you over first. It will meet your eyes and ping you with its sonar. It was exciting to know she was getting to know him inside and out! He was very much hoping that he passed inspection. Billy immediately started sending her love and pink beautiful energies from his heart. He wanted nothing from her. He simply observed and waited while sending love to her and all other beings of the seas!

In a moment she came back and brought him the golden leaf again! He was so excited he could hardly breathe. Although she was much

17

larger, he did not feel he was in any danger at all. In fact, perhaps this is the moment he had been waiting on for so long. He wondered what her name was, and as soon as he wondered, the word bubbles popped into his head. Bubbles! If your name is Bubbles, please give me a sign so that I know for sure, he thought. She immediately blew a beautiful round bubble at him and swam swiftly off!

It worked! She had read his mind and responded in a very real way. He was filled with surprise and awe. He was so excited that he flooded his mask again and choked on the water. It is very hard to smile with a mask on and laughter tends to flood a snorkel, but he really did not care! He swiftly put his head up and drained the salty water from his blue mask. Salt water did not burn his eyes the way that pool water did. Even so, he did not want to miss a thing. He put his snorkel back in his mouth and blew hard to clear it. It sounded just like the dolphins when they came up for air. When he laughed at the thought, he had to do it all over again. He knew it was an amazing start to an amazing adventure, and the beginning of his journey with the dolphins that he had been waiting for so long!

He saw a gray fin slowly coming toward him and again laid flat in the water to see what would happen next. Bubbles swam slowly toward him and met his eye. He saw and felt the energy coming from her and felt like he had just been transported into another dimension! She held his gaze for a very long time. It seemed like forever, and then she turned over. As he lay on his stomach face down in the water; she was on her back matching his position heart to heart! The energy that ran through him was so powerful and delightful that he almost could not bear it, and his heart opened wide to give and receive this beautiful pink loving energy. His eyes filled with tears as his heart filled with love. Just as he thought he could not love her anymore, she broke the energy and swam away. He heard in his mind a very soft loving voice that said, "Remember this experience. We will have many more. Remember my name. I am your teacher and friend if you like. We can teach you many things if you meet us here tomorrow. I am sending you Bubbles of Joy and will see you in your dreams tonight. See you tonight!"

She then disappeared. When he looked around, there were no dolphins to be seen and no colors flowing through the water. He could hear no clicks or chirps. "How did they go so fast?" he wondered as he swam back to shore. Although he did not want the experience with his friend to end, he was very excited about what had occurred and could not wait to go to sleep and see what he would dream! He felt the water getting shallower and warmer as he swam to shore and he waited until the last minute to stand up. It was always easier to move through the water as a swimmer. Walking just did not feel natural to him there. He took a moment to simply float in the water with his eyes closed and feel the warm sunshine on his face. It always felt so good to feel the difference between the coolness of the water and the warmness of the sun. He absorbed as much of the energy of the sun as he could. It simply felt good, like the love he felt from his father when he got a hug. Or, when he went to the Unity Church, how the preacher said God would feel.

Billy knew that time was passing and he needed to get home and eat supper. So he slowly left the water and started to amble home while looking for treasures of the sea and beautiful sea shells. It was getting cooler also. The sun showed him it was about 5 o'clock. He knew that he left the cottage around noon as soon as Mom released him from his chores. Where had the time gone? It seemed that he had only been in the water a few moments!

Skipping and dancing in the sand with excitement, Billy also looked down and around so that he would not miss any sea shell treasures. He always carried two bags that were netted, a bag to pick up any people trash that he found and a bag for his sea treasures. He was very careful if he found any sharp glass or fishing hooks. He did not like to get cut! The Park Ranger had told him that trash on the beach could kill or hurt birds and other animals if not removed. When he went to the animal rescue center, he saw the damage that trash could do and he never ever forgot it. He had learned not to ever throw trash in the water! Bottles and cans could trap animals. A lot of the trash they called "biodegradable" was not and would take almost forever to disappear. He tried to remind people of this when he was on the beach, but many did not seem to care and told him to run along. He had kept the number to the rescue center on the fridge in plain sight because if he ever found a hurt animal, he fully intended to help it. He was very kind hearted.

As Billy ambled on, at times jumping just like the dolphins for joy, he spotted a strange being standing on the beach. She had very, very large eyes and her skin was blue. Not just the blue that you turned when the water was too cold and you went in anyway. She was unmistakably very deep royal blue. This day was turning stranger and stranger! She looked at him and sent a beautiful blue beam that touched his heart and then she disappeared. She had no hair and her clothes looked like the clothes that he had seen in a book about the Romans. Her dress was blue and rippled in the light breeze flowing like the water. She was much taller and thinner than his mom. Billy rubbed his eyes to clear them and walked on.

This was not the first time he had seen a strange being. Many times he saw angels around people, and others that he did not recognize, but he thought they might have been family or friends of the people that they were with. They looked human. Sometimes the beings he saw were not with people but seemed to stay in a home or building.

Sometimes he saw animals or monsters around people. The people with monsters he avoided if he could. No one believed him when he tried to tell them, but that did not mean that he did not see them, just that they did not seem to be aware. It went right along with the colors that he saw around people. He had just learned to be silent about it.

But this was very different from those experiences, and this beautiful blue woman seemed to be trying to show herself to him.

He even saw bouncy bubbles simply floating in the air that seemed to show up around people that were especially happy or in prayer. The bubbles were various colors and really pretty, but he did not know what to make of that either! He wished he could talk to the bubble lady, even if just for a moment. He had a million questions and she seemed to know things that other people didn't. Billy sighed because he had learned to accept many things.

Chapter 5
The Magic Cottage

He knew he had to get home in a hurry, and he was very, very hungry! Swimming and the beach seemed to make him feel that way. Finally he arrived at the sidewalk to the door to his house. It was a very warm and cozy place and seemed to say just come on in! It was the smallest house on the beach. The sidewalk just invited you to come on in and take a seat. The house was filled with decorations that he and his mom had painted and made from the items he picked up on the beach. Sea shell wind chimes sparkled out their music in the air perfectly matching the shining sparkles on the beach. His mom had a small shop in the back of their house and sold many of these items to the tourists that came from near and far.

The screen slammed as Billy ran through the door. His mom came in from the back and kissed his cheek and hugged him. He wiped the pink paint off that always seemed to be on her face or hands from painting.

"Mom!" he said, "I am too old for that!" Billy's mom laughed and said, "Honey, you are never too old for a hug and kiss!" It made him squirmy, and he always pushed her away, but secretly he loved it and really loved his mom.

She was a tall blond woman who always had a smile on her lips and a twinkle in her sea blue eyes that matched his. Her hair was in a twist in the back and had lots of strands sticking out that tickled his face as she hugged him. She often said that she had mermaid hair that was naturally very curly and with a mind of its own! He thought she was beautiful. She always seemed to be laughing at some secret joke that only she knew, but it made her and everyone else very happy even when they were sad. There were lots of people who just could not stay away from her and the air of magic that followed her every where she went.

Most of the time, her clothes were covered with spots of every color of paint or dirt. It all depended on what she was painting or clay she was working on. Sometimes when he looked at her, he could see the faint outline of a mermaid tail around her legs and waist. Especially when she was complaining that her legs were tired and hurt was when the outline became clearer. She always smelled of the salt water and the ocean, and he noticed the smell of the ocean was getting stronger lately. She was wearing cut off blue jean shorts, old and blue like the sky, and a t-shirt that said "I Love Humans!" on it with a big whale staring at you. He thought it was the coolest shirt, and it made people laugh.

"I'm hungry!" Billy said, "What's for supper?"

"Your favorite," she replied with a tinkle in her voice.

"Shrimp?" he asked.

"Yep, so go wash the sand and salt off in the shower, and I will have it ready as soon as your dad gets home."

Billy's hair was plastered to his head with salt and sand and a bit itchy, so he really did not mind. Sand and salt also made his bathing suit scratchy and uncomfortable. He always felt better after his shower when he came back from the beach. Mom had to go through the whole beach return ritual, too. It was fun and comforting for both of them.

"I was just in the water," he yelled, then turned and ran for the shower just as mom threatened him with a towel smack and a smile.

When he entered the bathroom, he stopped with a start. He stood in the tiny bathroom and noticed suddenly that the entire bathroom looked like it was underwater! The walls were dark blue and his mom had painted murals on the wall with fish, sea weed and dolphins. He wondered when that had happened. Last time he was in the bathroom in the morning brushing his teeth, it was an ordinary normal bathroom with tiles on the white walls. There was even a shell shaped toilet now. The sink was like a shell too! In four hours? It was a very strange day indeed. He was not sure whether to ask her about it because, at times, things in the cottage shifted at random! No one else seemed to notice or cared when he asked because they seemed to think that it had always been that way.

He knew differently and was probably the only one who noticed. Sometimes he thought it was abnormally normal! He turned the shower on and noticed that even the handles were different. Now they had a little starfish on them, and the shower head was shaped like a sand dollar! The tile had changed from light blue to sea foam green and the shower curtain had huge dolphins on it. He liked it because the shower curtain turned the light into a green color that looked just like being under the water. He thought it was cool as he enjoyed his hot shower and then dried off with a new towel that he had never seen before. After hanging the towel on the shell decorated rack, he quickly got dressed and returned to the kitchen for supper.

Suddenly, their herd of Chihuahuas greeted him enthusiastically, barking and running around like crazy dogs! With all the high pitched excited barks, he could not even hear himself think! His mom rescued Chihuahuas and had 4 in the cottage right now. He could not remember when the house wasn't full of these beautiful little dogs they called pupples. He always greeted them in the same order. First he picked up Abbi aka Abbigale. She had lived a very adventurous life much different than most. She was black, tan and white- and the biggest of the bunch! He could not remember a time he did not have her, but she was getting old and could no longer see. At times, she coughed a lot and had to get medicine. She was still getting around pretty well, but his mom had said to be very gentle with her because she would not be around forever. "She is now 13 years old, and that is very very old for a puppy" his mom explained. Abbi and his mom had a very special relationship, and sometimes his mom looked at her with tears in her eyes and sadness.

Next came Tinker. Mom called her Tinker T Tiny, but her real name was Tinker Bell. His mom had saved her life at the age of three when she could not eat. At that time, she was just two lbs, but now she was a hefty four lbs. That was five years ago, so he had known her most of his life, too. She did not have many teeth, and her tongue stuck out all the time. Everyone told her she was the cutest thing as she danced and pranced her princess self all around the house! She was also black, tan and white- just like Abbi! Mom had to explain to everyone that they were not sisters. When his mom picked up Tinker, it was obvious that Tink was her favorite. His mom's heart always just beamed pink love like no other time, except when she went to see or swim with dolphins.

He next greeted the "pupples" as his parents called them. Six months ago, two tiny puppies arrived in a blanket and were only five weeks old. They were lots of fun as they toddled around the house. His mom was concerned that with Abbi getting so old, they needed new energy in the house. His mom said that she had asked Abbi and Tink, and they had agreed. Bella was called a "Blue". She was pretty gray/brown with green eyes and a little light brown nose. Izzy was jet black with a white chest. Her eyes were deep and black and seemed to shine like none of the others. At times, he could see tiny wings on her back in her energy field.

The pupples kept everyone very busy and entertained. One never knew what they would get into or drag up. Abbi was doing her best to get them trained before she left, but it was a challenge for all. Bella and Izzy had the same energies surrounding them and were never far away from each other. At times, it seemed that they were both the same, just in two different bodies. His mom called them "twin souls" and when he asked what she meant, she explained that sometimes more than one body can share the same soul. A soul is the energy that we really are. The energy is like the angels' but more solid. His mom had only planned to get one puppy, but when she saw both of them, there was no doubt that they couldn't be separated.

So, here came the pupples bouncing into their lives. Very seldom did any of the herd go outside as his mom was concerned about the fleas and, worst of all, big birds that could carry them off. So they had pads that they used as a bathroom, and every time they used the pad they got peanut butter. That was great until they figured out that they could get peanut butter anytime they liked by using the pad. So now, all four get peanut butter anytime they want. Actually, Billy had figured out that they were pretty smart. Perhaps the smartest of all animals since they had been training humans for a long time to feed them when they wanted, give them plenty of water and take care of all their needs. Seemed to him that they were smarter than even the wolves because they wanted for nothing most of the time. Some, like the pupples, got the best treatment in the world! He knew that they could see the beings that he saw because when an angel came into the house, the pupples greeted them just like they did him! When dark energy or a monster came in, they barked and ran off to hide under a bed. They even knew people. His mom and dad said everyone who came in had to pass the muster with the pupples. If the pupples did not like whomever came in, they were not invited back. Dogs are very perceptive!

Billy wandered to the window. He couldn't believe his eyes. There were new people moving in next door! He watched carefully as they unloaded a big orange truck. A little girl about his age was standing beside the truck holding a stuffed dolphin and clutching it to her heart. He could tell she was excited and uneasy at the same time. Billy thought she held the dolphin to her heart to comfort herself. She seemed shy and uneasy as she stood alone hopping on one foot and then the other. Her mother came and got her and hurried her into the house. Her mother did not seem very nice to the little girl, but perhaps it was because her mother was busy as she boldly gave directions to everyone there.

The front door slammed shut, and Billy heard the bells ring. There were bells on every door in their cottage because his mom wanted to be able to tell when someone came in no matter where she was. Often the doors and windows were open to let the sea breeze in, and customers and friends wandered in often. His mom always said as she breezed through a room, "If you believe you are safe, then you are. The more locks and closed doors you have, the more you prove to the world you are not safe, and something will be created to prove it true." She was always saying crazy things like that. He had seen the news and sometimes was afraid, but nothing had ever happened to him and nothing was ever missing from the house. So he was giving it a chance. He never had to carry a key like other kids, and he liked that part. He had never seen a single door to their home locked at any time. Even the sign for the shop said, "Open 24 hours a day! Come on in!" It just made everyone feel better to see one place that was so fearless and filled with love!

His dad always came into the house like a hurricane filled with energy and love for his family. He always took the time to greet and hug everyone. He sailed boats and worked on engines. He smelled a bit like fuel, burnt oil and a lot like sweat. After kissing his wife, hugging his son and greeting the pupples, he headed to the shower to get clean for supper. Billy wondered if his dad would notice the difference in the bathroom. He hadn't had a chance to mention it to his mom yet.

Shrimp was cooking and he could smell it. Billy could not wait for supper. He was really hungry! So he played with the puppies until it was ready and dad got out of the shower. He looked out the window at the house next door and noticed a new car in the driveway. All the windows and doors were shut tight, and there was no sign of life over there. But upstairs he could see half a face with blond hair peeping out the window curtain. The energy of that house felt very heavy. Oh well, he thought, let's give it a chance and see how they are. He hoped the little girl he saw felt better now, but it did not feel that way.

Billy took a deep breath and turned just as his dad left the bathroom in a cloud of steam and went to the bedroom to get out of the towel and dress for supper. When his dad sat down on the over stuffed comfortable couch in the den, he asked Billy how his day was. Billy looked down and said, "It was ok." He was not ready to share what had happened yet. He was not sure his dad would understand. Billy was not sure he understood all of it yet either. He treasured his experiences, and he wanted to keep them to himself until he could sort them through.

"Did you go to the beach?" Dad asked.

"Of course," Billy replied.

"Find anything interesting?"

"Not really, just shells."

About that time, they heard his mom ring out in her musical voice, "Supper's ready!"

They both got up and went to the table that was covered with a bright red tablecloth and looked very inviting!

Billy could hardly finish his meal, he was so excited about his day so far! He was eager to go to bed and see what his dreams would be because Bubbles said she would see him then. His parents looked at him funny through the whole meal because they knew something was up. He wolfed down his food and asked if he could be excused. His mom said "Of course". He went to his bedroom and put on his pajamas. His mom was washing the dishes from supper when Billy walked in. He padded across the floor in his dolphin slippers and hugged her goodnight.

"What in the world is going on with you?" his mom asked with a laugh. "You never want to go to bed. Now you are in your pajamas with your teeth brushed, and it is only 7 o'clock!"

"Oh, I'm just sleepy tonight from swimming in the ocean," Billy said. He watched her washing the dishes and saw that she was fascinated with the soap bubbles. There was something about the bubbles that was right at the corner of his mind but would not come out. They were strangely sparkled and shiny and almost magical! He stood there lost in thought for a moment as fascinated with the bubbles as his mom was.

His mom asked, "Are you still here, Billy?" as she noticed him just standing and staring at the soap bubbles in the sink. He excitedly ran upstairs to go to bed, wondering how he would ever get to sleep. He thought this is better than Christmas and waiting for the reindeer and Santa. One hundred times better!

Chapter 6
The Pupples Speak

The pupples seemed to catch his excitement. Izzy and Bella ran with him and were more excited than usual. Every night his family watched one hour of TV and then watched the Chihuahua races. The pupples raced to and fro at random through the house at full speed, bumping into everything, biting and barking at each other. Usually Abbi and Tinker watched from a far, but every once in a while, they joined in the fray. You never knew what they would do, but it was always fun and great entertainment. There were puppy toys all over the house and they grappled with them at random. Tonight Bella had their dolphin and brought it to Billy. She looked at Billy as she laid it at his feet. Izzy was busy pulling and tugging at his pajama leg. Bella was more laid back and enjoyed her nightly petting from everyone. Izzy was much too busy for that. Sometimes he called them Busy Izzy and Bella Blue Baby. They definitely knew their names!

Billy went to the bathroom to get a glass of water to put beside his bed. The pupples all sat quietly outside the door and waited for him to finish getting the water, then followed him down the hall like body guards. Each pupple had its own bed, but sometimes when they were very good or if there was a thunderstorm, they got to sleep with someone. When he opened his door, they all trouped in and waited beside his bed. This was unusual. He did not remember this ever happening before. They lined up in a row and looked at him. Good Grief! He wondered what was going on. He asked out loud, "What do you guys want?" They all at once turned around like soldiers and put their front paws on the bed to be let up. That had never happened before either. Suddenly a small voice came from Bella in English. "Yes, we want up!" He could hear it clearly in his mind and thought it was his imagination that he could hear it out loud. Before he had only heard yips and barks and Izzy had not even found her inner bark yet! She could only manage small squeaks that were her attempts at barking.

33

"Well, we aren't standing here all day," Billy heard from Abbi in a deep growly voice. "My legs are getting tired."

Tinker said in her tinkly voice, "Would you hurry up and get in the bed already." Bella turned her head and just looked at him. Billy was so surprised he just sat down on the floor.

"Mom, Dad, come look at this!" He shouted at once.

Immediately the pupples started acting normally again with Abbi fussing at the pupples and Izzy and Bella running around with toys. Tinker turned and walked to her bed to lie down. Everything was back to normal by the time his mother arrived wiping her hands on a red dishtowel. His dad hurried in right behind her.

"What have the pupples done now?" they asked.

"Nothing, they quit" Billy said with disappointment. He had hoped they could see it, too. His mom and dad gave each other a look and went back to the kitchen and living room respectively.

When they left, Bella looked at him reproachfully and said with her inner bark, "What did you do that for?" They all lined up in front of him again.

"This is for only you to see!" said Tinker, dancing in her tinker way.

"We communicate all the time for people who can hear. But the dolphins gave us permission to really speak to you in English so we can help guide and protect you through this journey," said Abbi in her growly cranky voice.

"Can you hear us now?" Izzy asked.

Tinker sang out, "Can I have some peanut butter?"

And Abbi barked, "Just where is my bone?" in that particular growl she used when she was addressing the pupples. All at once, a million questions went through his mind, more than he could possibly ask at one time.

"Have you guys been able to talk like this all along?" he asked them.

"Of course!" they chorused together.

Tinker shared, "We can always speak to those who are listening, sometimes out loud, but most of the time in a quiet voice in your head. We send pictures to people, but alas, most humans don't hear us. They just are not listening. We also get our messages across in other ways."

Abbi added, "How many times has your mom bragged about me for being able to scratch on the cabinet under the sink to get water when she forgets to fill our water bowl? Sometimes I even have to scratch on the bathtub. I know where water comes from. I watch you guys all the time!"

"Good point," Billy responded. Izzy ran off into another direction.

Abbi cried out at her, "Come back now."

Izzy laid her ears back and slunk back to her place saying, "Sorry, short attention span. I am a puppy you know." Everyone laughed, including Billy!

Billy explained his experience he had with Bubbles to the puppies as they sat quietly and listened.

"We knew that," said Tink. "We know everything. We watch you all the time even when you are not home. How do you think we know when your dad turns the corner and is getting close to home? You have seen us do it a thousand times."

"I often wondered about that," Billy said. "Ok, so you guys can talk, huh?" Billy was finally letting their communications sink in.

"Yip," were the four replies at once.

"Well, Bubbles told me she would visit me in my dreams tonight and I can't wait to see what's next, so what do you guys want?" Billy asked.

"All of us won't fit in your bed, so go get our beds and put them in here so we can guard you well tonight," said Abbi. Billy got up and did what he was instructed in order to get set up for the next adventure.

"Smarties!" he thought.

Billy returned to mayhem with Izzy and Bella playing rough, tumbling and gleefully pulling each other across the floor by their tails and cheeks at random. There were lots of growls, yet full of fun and play.

He wondered for a moment if it had really happened when Tinker said in her princess like fashion, "Well don't just stand there. Put our beds down and go get our blankets." At that moment he was sure. He went and got the blankets to go with the beds and everyone settled down and curled around the bed with Izzy and Bella in one bed, Tinker and Abbi in the other. "Why did I have to get all four beds for you if you are only using two beds?" He asked them.

"We just wanted to see if you understood us. You humans are a real challenge to communicate with, you know," Abbi said. "You just don't listen, you are very slow and are very hard to train!"

Billy retorted, "Huh?", as he crawled into bed. He would have been irritated and insulted if he had not been so amused and astounded at the turn of events.

It only took a moment for him to fall asleep, even though he thought he was too excited to sleep! The moment he closed his eyes, Bubbles showed up.

Chapter 7

Bubbles in Dreamtime

She was there, hovering near his bed, and then suddenly Bubbles popped up facing him. She was laughing!

"Are you ready to go?" she asked with her wide dolphin grin. "We have been waiting so long for this to happen! I want to introduce you to my friends." Very excitedly, she said, "Grab my fin and let's go!"

Billy took hold of her fin with his left hand and that put them side by side, rising up ever so slowly into the air. The surprise was all his when he accidentally let go and immediately fell back on to the bed.

"Carp," Billy shouted out in surprise; "I thought this would be easy."

Bubbles rejoined, "Don't worry Billy, you'll get used to it. Just climb on to my back." Not knowing how this was all going to work, he slowly climbed up on to her back, and away they went. He could see the roof of the cottage as they passed over it and the gulf was lit with phosphorous as the waves gently crashed onto the shore.

Gently coming down from above the rooftops, Bubbles softly landed on the sand. Bubbles looked at Billy and asked him if he was ready for an adventure and meet her friends. With a big smile, Billy shouted out, "Of course I am!" Bubbles rose weightlessly from the sand and said, "Get ready then, and follow me into the water."

"I'll get wet, and I can't breathe under water!" exclaimed Billy.

"Yes you can. Watch this!" said Bubbles with excitement. Billy felt her in front of him and suddenly it felt as if a beam of light went from her heart to his. It was so strong it nearly took his breath away. It was a frequency she told him was the "Blue Diamond DNA Download" beam. Billy could feel the surge hit his heart, then spread quickly all over his body and put him in a blue bubble of energy.

"I just made you a dolphin," Bubbles giggled. "Now, when you go on our trips you can change at will to be your beautiful dolphin self and go into my world easily!" "Come on!" she cried.

He still looked like his old self, just a bit more shimmery in his energy, but he felt tingles all over like when soda tickles his nose. "What an adventure this will be," he thought. He walked to the water with Bubbles floating above the sand right beside him. The water was cool and dark blue with sparkles that looked like stars with a light of their own. He looked back and saw the "Blue Lady" standing off behind him smiling from ear to ear. "Oh!" said Bubbles, "You will meet her later. You will love her, but hurry on. We don't have much time!"

He waded slowly into the water. As he did, a big blue bubble covered him from the top of his head to the bottom of his feet. He was dry as a bone! His head went under water, and he could still breathe. This was amazing to Billy. He started to swim like a dolphin and suddenly he had a tail! "How? What?" Billy questioned this in his mind, stopped in surprise and slowly sank to the bottom in the sand. Bubbles swam up beside him and said, "Humans used to be dolphins and dolphins used to be humans. We chose to go back into the water, and you guys chose to stay on land. I think we made the better choice!"

A small golden star fish jumped into his pocket! "What on earth are you doing?" he asked the small starfish. The starfish giggled and wiggled in delight!

"My name is Perfect," she said as she peaked up from his shirt pocket with a grin. "Whenever you do something amazing, you receive a gold star like you get in school." Billy gently took her in his hand, and she immediately jumped to the outside of his pocket to ride with him. "Good job of trusting Bubbles," said the little star fish with a smile! "You get an A and a gold starfish for the night!"

Just then a sea turtle swam by. He slowly glided up to Billy and met his eyes. "Hi! My name is David," he said. "I came by to remind you to slow down and be ever so present so that you do not miss a thing on this wonderful adventure. Whenever you need to be 'pulled back together', so to speak, just call my name, and I will come," David said this in a slow turtle kind of way.

"Pulled back together?" Billy asked nervously. "Am I coming apart?" he asked afraid.

"No, silly. There will be many changes to your energy patterns as you receive the gifts we have to offer. Whenever you get overwhelmed, just call, and I can help," said David the Turtle.

"Great," said Billy. "Don't have a clue what you are talking about, but I will be sure to call you if I need your help." Billy was actually just playing along with the beautiful turtle. He really did not have a clue what his new friend was talking about.

Bubbles and Billy swam along under the water, and Bubbles allowed Billy to take his time to get used to swimming with his tail. First, Billy could only swim to the right. Then he could only swim to the left and upside down at that. It was a whole new sensation to breathe under water and swim with a tail! It was a good thing that he had taught himself how to do the dolphin kick with his legs because at least he had an idea of how to swim up and down with his body and legs together. Billy was amazed at how clearly he could see under the water without his mask. He thought this was really cool and hoped he could do it later when he was not dreaming. He watched the water light up with little geometric jelly-like creatures that looked as if they had blue or green tiny wires in them as they floated by. They seemed to gather around him and gently light his way.

The bottom was covered with brown fuzzy sand dollars, and he could see the trails they left behind as they moved along the bottom. Billy shouted, "Hey, what is that?"

"Oh," said Bubbles, "did you know that sand dollars come out of the sand at night and crawl around? What you find on the beach is the skeleton of a living being. We use them to communicate with others like cell phones, and you can use them to communicate with us when you need. The sand dollars work along with other shells to help us all with our communications in the sea. Sand dollars are also a sign of abundance and money. Many times when we are giving the gift of abundance to a human on the beach, we send them a sand dollar to pick up and hold and take home with them! Most humans don't get it, but Seasea, the dolphin woman you saw earlier, does. We send her lots of sand dollars, and she finds them where others have just looked. Cool huh?" asked Bubbles.

Billy was thankful that he and Bubbles swam slowly so he could get used to his beautiful tail. Billy was swimming randomly from side to side, and his jerky motions were not as fluid as Bubbles'. He was learning how to swim not just like a dolphin, but as one. He noticed that they were going farther and farther out, and the water was getting deeper and deeper. Out that far, the water was much bluer in color. Jelly fish slowly drifted by, and the schools of fish were ever present hanging around any piece of trash on the bottom or just slowly swimming parallel to the shore. They all moved in a dance, swirling in unison, darting this way and that.

Suddenly it struck him. HE HAD A TAIL! A beautiful tail! A very strong tail! He just had to take a look! It was covered in brilliant blue green scales that actually felt soft to the touch – like the Mahi-Mahi he caught once when he and his dad were out in his dad's boat on a fishing trip. Billy's tail tapered into a beautiful wide fin at the bottom that was horizontal and was kind of transparent. It was scalloped but not up and down like a fish, but horizontal like a dolphin. He noticed coming out of his back was a large fin, just like a dolphin's.

"Hey, this is cool," he thought. Billy was so entranced with his new body that he hadn't noticed that he had sunk to the bottom in the sand! He decided to play with this new body and see what it would do. He swam straight up and leaped out of the water.

"WHOO, this is AMAZING!" Billy thought with jubilation. Up and down, round and round he went until he was kind of tired. Bubbles swam back by his side and met his eye.

"Are you finished now?" she asked. He slowly settled down and swam by her side again.

"I thought you made me a dolphin, but I have a mermaid tail. What happened?" asked Billy.

"People swim much easier with a mermaid tail. Plus you also have Mer blood in your family!" said Bubbles with a smile. That stopped Billy in his tracks! He had wondered about that...Oh! but there were so many other questions he had.

"How do dolphins swim so fast?" Billy asked Bubbles.

"Dolphin can do so much more than humans understand," Bubbles offered. She then blew a beautiful bubble and swam through it. "We are masters at sound and vibration and traveling in and out of dimensions. We are multidimensional and can hold any vibration or borrow any vibration we need. The only other beings who can do that are humans. Other animals can do this too, but it depends where their souls are from. These abilities are usually in people's pets as they come in service to teach humanity different lessons. Puppies are really masters, just in little puppy bodies. Listen closely to them because they are very wise. I will teach you how to do this too Billy, but first, there are some 'Beings of the Sea' who are waiting to meet you. I am also going to teach you how to hold any vibration." Bubbles was really excited as they swam out to greet them.

Chapter 8

Friends of the Sea

Billy sensed a huge energy coming slowly toward him. It felt as if he had electricity flowing through every cell of his body, and his skin, now turned into scales, vibrated in a slow pulsating rhythm. He swam behind Bubbles feeling a bit afraid and timid. Suddenly, a huge humpback whale was swimming nearby.

"Oh my goodness!" he thought with astonishment. Billy had never seen one before. The frequencies that he felt were amazing. He imagined it was like being in a big, dark, fuzzy hole but not in a scary way. Just like he felt when he was holding his mom's Buddha statue. Bubbles, David and Billy froze in awe as the huge whale swam by a couple of times. Billy could see that the humpback's eye was bigger then he was. As the whale swam toward them, Billy came face to face with one of its eyes.

"Hi. My name is Humphrey. What is your name, little one?" the humpback whale thundered. At first, Billy was frozen to the spot! Then he shook his head and answered timidly, "Billy".

"Nice to meet you, Billy," said Humphrey with a big toothy grin, "You will be meeting several others tonight along with us. Are you ready?" he asked kindly.

Just then, a small orca swam to them. Rapidly, she went round and round Humphrey and then stopped beside Billy. "You are not going to eat either one of us are you?", Billy said with a concerned look.

"No, no, of course not," Ora the orca claimed with a smile. "I am also one of your guides, and we are not allowed to eat those we protect. Anyway, seals are my favorites, and you don't look anything like a seal." Billy placed his hand on the orca's smooth black and white skin. It felt cool and wet, like a hard boiled egg after the shell is removed and ready to be dipped in salt to eat.

Then a swiftly moving shape flashed by that went to the surface and leapt right out of the water, spinning in joy as she went.

"Spinner, you are here," said Bubbles. "Glad you could make it! This is Billy." Billy was now getting a bit nervous. All these beautiful beings were much bigger than he – beautiful but bigger!

"Billy, are you ready to come to our city under the sea?" asked Bubbles.

"Yes," said Billy shyly. The whole group surrounded him and they started to move to deeper water. It seemed like they swam forever into darker and bluer water and passed by several coral reefs that all had human faces carved into them. "That is not natural," said Billy. "Just how did those faces get here?"

"Dolphins have art, and we do carving with sound and vibrations," explained Bubbles. Some of the carvings looked familiar to him as they passed by.

"We all carve out our favorite humans," Bubbles continued. He saw Seasea's beautiful face in one of them with sea fans gently moving in the curves around her smile. He went over for a closer look. The details were amazing! Tiny fish picked the carving clean, and a big green Moray eel had a home right beside the carving as if to guard it. He could have spent all night there studying the carvings and decided he wanted to come back later. Just as he was swimming away, he caught a glimpse of his mother's beautiful face looking at him from the coral! No, it could not be. He wondered about it. Then he decided that he had been mistaken.

They swam for a while, and when he looked to his right, he could see dolphins busily building ropes of blue energy using phosphorus. They were following the latest phosphorus rope that the dolphins had created. It was like a line of twinkling blue lights. Then they came to a wall. It had every coral and sea fan that he had ever read about with seahorses, fish, crabs, small orange striped shrimp and more than he could see in hours in a one foot space. There was so much to see and look at, and it seemed to Billy that the wall was teaming with life. As they got closer, it turned clearer until they swam through the iridescent film. It tickled his skin like goose bumps as they swam through it one by one.

"A city, a real city!" Billy gasped with his mouth wide open in astonishment. He was seeing streets, buildings, and houses, all in sand, with crystal and coral and of every beautiful color he had ever seen! They swam slowly down the street, and the dolphins, whales and fish swam right by. He was able to stand and swim because his legs or fins appeared as needed and without effort or thought.

"Here is the first thing that we would like to show you, and we have someone we would love for you to meet. As a matter of fact, you have already seen her, you just did not get a chance to meet her," said Bubbles. Billy's curiosity was up, and he was on full alert.

Chapter 9

The Healing Chamber

Bubbles, Billy and Spinner slowly swam up to a big gray building that had Cetacean Healing Chamber on the outside, in big red letters made of coral. Bubbles touched the doors with her rostrum, and they automatically opened. Silently and seriously, they all filed in, one by one. This was a definite shift in their energies. They went down a long hallway and at the end of it, there was the healing chamber. Bubbles, Billy and Spinner filed in one at a time. There was no one there! "Just wait for a moment," said Ora the Orca. They sat quietly, and Billy studied the room. It was circular, tall and had a domed ceiling with a hole in the middle like a light shining down. An amphitheater is what they called it. In circular rows, there were benches to sit on. The benches were light blue and glowed with a light all their own. He sat on one, and looking around, he noticed a glow throughout the whole room. There was a table in the middle where the light that came in through the ceiling hole and illuminated it. More and more dolphins and whales were coming in quietly. They were all different sizes and shapes.

When it appeared that every one had assembled, the blue lady, whom he had seen on the beach, came in carrying a little girl, hanging limply and draped over the blue lady's arm. It looked like she was sleeping. Billy could see bruises on her face, and one of her arms hung at a strange angle – even her feet were bruised and dirty. Quietly Billy asked, "What happened?"

With tears on her face, Bubbles said, "Some children choose to have family's that are not very nice to them so that they can hone their skills in extrasensory perception and learn what not to do. Not all moms and dads are nice people like yours."

"This girl," she said quietly, "is your next door neighbor. Her name is Sandy. Her father got very angry about the move to the new house near you and took it out on her. She is very important to us, and we visit her often, and most times this is how she comes to us.

The blue lady is named Neema. She is from the seven sisters' star system called Sirus and the planet Delphinus. It is a magical water planet where the dolphins originally came from. It is a blue star planet that is in another dimension of light. Many a time, Sandy would have been permanently hurt or maimed, but Neema has been taking care of her for years. Sandy's parents can't understand how she heals so quickly, but they are glad of it because there are no hospital visits to explain. Now be still and watch quietly".

Neema laid Sandy very gently on the table. The room was completely silent. From all around the chamber, the dolphins and whales of every size and shape swam quietly and formed a circle around Sandy. There were humans in the circle also. He recognized Seasea, his mom and many others, as they quietly joined in the circle.

They all closed their eyes and breathed very deeply. The humans had their hands on their hearts. Then, they dropped their hands, and a vibrant blue energy seemed to leap from their hearts to form a bubble around Sandy. Slowly, as the bubble got bigger and enveloped them all, they stepped out of the bubble and stood outside the circle. A beam of light came from each and every heart, like laser beams, directed at Sandy. Every beam was a different color, but it all felt like love. It was so beautiful. It brought tears to Billy's eyes. There were pink beams from the whale hearts, green from the humans and blue from the dolphins. It thrilled Billy to see the dolphins standing on their tails and holding hands with flippers outside the bubble.

There were mermaids and mermen, green beings and yellow sun like beings that were so bright they were difficult to look at. He even saw a manatee!

He watched in amazement as Sandy's arm straightened out and the bruises faded in moments. Her hair grew shiny, and pink filled her cheeks and lips where before she was pale and colorless. She was taking deep breaths where before she could hardly breathe. This went on quietly for several minutes. Sandy opened her eyes and sat up with a giggle! "Wow!" she said wiggling her fingers and toes in delight! "I feel great! Thank you all!" He could see others waiting outside the chamber to bring children, sick whales and others into the chamber. Many humans were there.

Sandy jumped up and ran to Billy. She had to slip between a big orca and three dolphins to get to him. He glanced behind her to see others being brought to the healing table. "Hi!" Sandy exclaimed. "You are the little boy I saw next door at the cottage with the shells to the side of it."

Billy asked Sandy, "Do you have friends here?"

"Of course I have," said Sandy. "I have to come here often. I have two friends here. One is yellow, like the sun. Although he looks like a lion, he walks on two feet. His name is Solera. My other best friend is another blue lady with no hair. Her name is Almera. They take care of me when I call them. My dad drinks a lot and my mom is very scared of the world and him. They really don't know how to love, so they get angry and I get hit a lot. I never know when it is coming but I always feel better when I come here." She was so excited she was having trouble speaking quietly.

"What is your name?" She asked.

"Billy," he replied, "Billy Sandwalker".

Billy and Sandy slipped quietly into another room. There were many windows all around, and they were decorated with shells. They could still see into the chamber. This room was small and had a coral table with soft spongy chairs around it. There was a beautiful iridescent shell fountain in the middle of the room. Water ran from seemingly nowhere to fill the shell. It was clear, clean sparkling fresh water for them to drink. Sandy picked up a shell shaped cup and drank deeply from the fountain.

One after another, they watched children and adults from every nation and beings from every ocean coming through the great door that lead into the room they were in. At times, the room would get bigger and large groups would all come in at the same time. Her friends, Almera and Solera, came in and sat quietly with them.

"Hello," they both said together, "nice to meet you Billy!" Billy instantly remembered them. When he was very small, his parents told him that Almera and Solera did not exist and they were imaginary friends he just made up. They were actually his teachers. His parents could not keep up with him and all his questions. Almera and Solera kept up with his questions very well. He recalled their visits and remembered them taking him to different places in the woods and speaking with him. It started before he could walk. He finally had to ask them to stop telling him so much and taking him on fantastic trips when he was four years old. It was worrying his parents too much because he seemed to disappear from the back yard and escape all fences and end up in the woods or other places that took his parents hours to find him. They asked him if they could start seeing him again, just not taking him away, and Billy agreed. With the reintroduction, Almera and Solera smiled and quietly left the room.

Chapter 10
Bubble School

Bubbles and Spinner swam into the room where all were gathered. "Come on! Come on!" they said. "You are late for our class!" Billy climbed onto Bubbles and Sandy climbed onto Spinner and away they went. It was like riding a very swift horse, except there was no wind or sense of movement. With no water flying by, there was an odd sensation to the ride as if he was being swept through a big vacuum. He was too busy holding onto her fin to formulate any questions right then.

But in his mind, he heard Bubbles say, "We are masters at frequencies, and we just move the water out of the way as we swim. It gives us space to swim into without the water resistance. Cool, huh?" Billy thought it was amazing how Bubbles could read his mind and answer questions as he thought of them. It was a much faster way to communicate!

Billy and Sandy hung on for dear life! They moved very quickly. They went into a large school building that looked just like his school on land, except it was all made from pink conch shells! They hurried into the classroom as class was already underway. It was being taught by a huge gray octopus with the end of each of her arms wrapped around a piece of chalk! She pointed chalk in every direction as she was saying "And now we will learn how to be safe where ever we are."

As Billy looked around the room, he realized there had to be at least 30 to 40 people, each with a pencil and pad before them. He was again so astonished that he had to clench his jaw and close his mouth. He looked at Sandy, and she looked just as amazed. Her eyes were as big as saucers.

"Hurry, hurry, take your seat!" said Olga the Octopus! Just as they took their seats, Olga said, "Ok, now get up and form a circle."

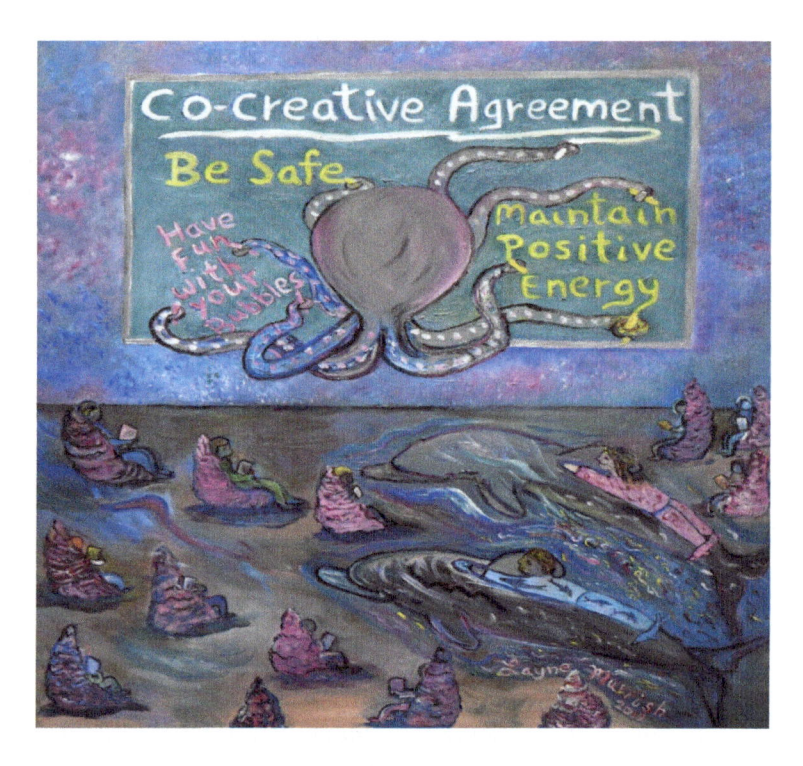

Everyone quickly moved the chairs back to the walls and formed a lopsided egg shape. "No! No! No!" said Olga, reaching out to adjust everyone with all eight arms. She sat in the middle of the circle and started to give instructions to the group. All the people in the room sat down with the papers she had given them and pencils in hand.

Loudly, and with grand enthusiasm, Olga announced, "Here is what we will learn today – I will teach you the dolphin tips and rules for stormy waters and shark pools. I call it 'Dolphin Rules for Shark Pools', but you need to know that every being in the ocean has its place and every being of the ocean has its own job to do."

"Dolphins and the beings of the seas want to teach people a better way to live," said Olga. Her arms were going in every direction. Billy found it a bit distracting. He always had problems sitting in a desk for any length of time. His teachers said he was a daydreamer and did not pay attention in class, but the truth of the matter was he just found school boring.

They all had a copy of the rules and had to sign them and pass them back up to the front of the class. Billy really wanted this to be over with. Dolphin school was not what he expected. He impatiently waited for the next part.

Olga took this very seriously and looked at everyone in the class. "If you understand, please raise your hand." Every hand in the class rose quickly. They all wanted to get to the fun exercises! It was a lot to take in, especially all the information that they had to read in the copy of the Dolphin Rules for Shark Pools.

"Now for the Fun Part!" said Olga. "We are going to do the 'I Am' Bubble Exercise. First, put your 'I Am' circle on the floor."

Billy looked at the papers he was holding, and there was a circle of paper with his name on it just like magic. The circle had a dolphin on it, and around the edges was printed 'I am Billy'. He quickly put the circle on the floor and waited to see what came next!

Olga continued, "Create a 'Bubble of Energy' by putting your hands out and stating out loud: 'Bubble of (Your Name) activate.' If you do not feel the energy, then just pretend that it is there. If you visualize energy, you will see it forming. If you hear energy, you will hear it activating. You will be playing with statements in this bubble. Your job is to just observe your bubble as you work with these statements. So when you feel this bubble is fully activated, step into it or bring it over you. Now you are ready to start playing with the bubbles."

Olga put two of her many arms out and showed them how to create the bubble.

Billy put his hands out about four feet wide and brought them slowly together while saying, "I am Billy. Bubble activate!" When he moved his hands to about a foot apart, he definitely felt something. It was a tingling and very light airy feeling. But it was really there!

He played with it a while, and then something more amazing happened. He suddenly could see the bubble forming in his hands!

It was light blue and shimmery and felt cool to the touch. He was so startled he almost dropped it. He has seen bubbles of energy but had no idea he could make one!

Olga then told the class to make the bubble much larger.

Billy asked the bubble to get larger and it did. He was amazed and fascinated. Now this was the kind of school he wanted to be in. This was fun!

Olga told the class to make the bubble as big as they were and to step into it.

Billy asked the bubble to get larger, and lo and behold, it got much bigger! When he stepped into the bubble, it felt like stepping into a cool breeze. He could tell when he was inside without a doubt. He stepped into it and out of it several times just to make sure. He looked around, and everyone in the class was stepping in and out of different colored bubbles!

"Class, class," Olga said, "when you are ready, step into the bubbles and stay there." The class waited expectantly, after they each stepped into their own bubbles. "Now say out loud: All energies that are not my own, please leave my bubble now," Olga instructed.

The whole class said, "All energies that are not my own, please leave my bubble now."

Billy saw a bunch of energy that looked like swirling fog, leave his bubble and float gently upward toward the ceiling. Billy could see that the room was full of light beings floating outside the bubbles of each person in the class. Angels, teachers, relatives and everyone he could imagine were standing just outside everyone's bubbles, and lots of energy flowed toward a light that appeared in the corner of the room.

"What you are seeing," said Olga "is negative energy that is going to be transformed and brought back to you later. Just take a deep breath and let yourself feel your own energy without any interference for a moment."

Everyone's bubble in the room looked bright, clear and sparkly. Some people still had a bit of dark energy in their bubbles, and Olga told them, "The dolphins are going to come around and ping your bubbles to finish clearing them out for those of you who need a bit of help. Everyone, please take a deep breath and ask the energy again to leave your bubble and tap gently on your collarbone, or over your heart to help let the energy go."

Billy saw Bubbles come and check on him and Sandy. Bubbles pinged some places on Sandy's bubble, and when Sandy gently tapped her chest, the energy floated to the light as it was released.

Billy saw Sandy take a deep breath and smile. Now her bubble was a very clear pink.

Olga continued, "Now ask your dolphins, teachers and guardian angels that share your light and love to come back into your bubbles."

Everyone stated out loud: "All energies of light and love please come back into my bubble!"

All the angels, masters and beings of light gently floated back into each person's bubble. For many in the room there was a look of relief. Billy found his bubble was lonely without his angels and dolphins inside, and it felt very different when he was all alone in his bubble. The difference was amazing!

Olga continued, "In order to find out who you are and what your energy is, you have to find out who you are not. Ask the guides to step in and out several times and play with it so that you can tell the difference."

Everyone played with this for a while, and the angels and guides seemed to really enjoy teaching the people in the class this lesson. Every person looked a bit different and amazed that they could do this!

"Are you ready for the next step?" Olga asked.

Everyone in the class waited expectantly.

"Now close your eyes and say this statement and breathe it into your bubbles!"

"I am safe." said Olga.

They all put their hands over their hearts and closed their eyes.

Each one quietly said, "I am safe." The room grew very still and quiet for a moment.

Everyone took a deep breath together. It was amazing to see everyone's face relax, and for just one moment, everyone really felt safe.

Sandy looked completely different! She was relaxed and happy, which Billy was very glad to see. Olga said, "It is time to give each other a hug and congratulate yourselves for a job well done!"

Gold starfish came into the room and jumped onto everyone's chest. The whole room was filled with happiness and joy. What a difference! Billy was amazed and could not wait for what was next!

"When you are finished with the bubble exercises, know you carry your beautiful energy every where you go. When your bubble is clear, you are clear. And add joy to it, and add love to it. Play with this, and make it your own," said Olga with a smile.

"A couple of last thoughts," Olga said. "Remember that whatever you resist will persist. Energy is just that, energy. When you observe and breathe through energy it automatically shifts and changes. Have fun with this! Ask the dolphins and your angels to help you if you get stuck, and spirit dolphins will come and help you."

"The next thing we are going to do is for everyone to form a bubble in between your hands again. It can be any color." Billy's bubble was light blue. Sandy's was golden yellow. As he looked around the circle, the bubbles were every color of the rainbow.

"Now turn to the one next to you, and put your hands through the bubbles to cut them in half and see how it feels!" It was a moment of chaos when no one knew which way to turn to get a partner!

"OK! OK! OK!" cried Olga. "Everyone turn to the right to get a partner."

Every one turned to the right, and no one had a partner. You could hear the frustration in Olga's voice as she said, "Well, that didn't work either! Count around the circle one, two then…Come on people… chop chop!" she shouted as she clapped four times with her mighty arms! Billy heard the words one, two, one, two as theywent around the circle. "Now, ones and twos get together!" said Olga, "And form a little bubble between your hands."

Each person carefully and slowly moved a hand, kind of like a karate chop, between each other's hands cutting the bubbles in half. It was like moving through an electric current. It tickled Billy's palm and felt sometimes cold and sometimes hot depending on which hand he used.

"Now, when you are complete, pour your bubbles from hand to hand!" Olga continued. It moved just like an old slinky toy Billy used to own. It was not his imagination! He could truly feel something. It was amazing!

"Now, get back into the circle, and pass the bubbles from one to another around the circle adding a color or an emotion to the bubbles," Olga went on to say. Billy watched with fascination as the bubble got bigger and bigger and turned colors – green, white, spiritual purple, all filled with joy, love, dance, play. One person even put in chocolate chip cookies, and you could smell them!

"Now, duplicate this large bubble around the circle so that each of you is holding one," Olga instructed. Each formed his bubble, and they all looked just alike.

Olga stated, "Now, lift your bubbles above your heads, and throw them to the center." It was the most amazing thing as all the bubbles burst at one time, and the colors and smells and feelings splashed back over each of them splashing them with little bubbles of energy. It was like the most amazing shower you had ever taken.

"Now," said Olga, "breathe in these gifts that everyone put into the bubbles, and you will hold them and share them with everyone you meet from your heart!"

She then taught them how to send the bubbles from their hands around the circle, and each had a chance to try it. Each person's bubble had a different feel and color, and there was no mistaking it when it came to them. Billy was quite amazed. He didn't think Olga was allowing enough time for this as he was having a blast. But he was in her class and knew she had to continue with her teaching.

"All the number ones, make a line. All the number twos, make a line and face each other. Quick, quick, our time is fleeting!" Olga said as she swiftly moved people with all eight arms into the proper places.

"The next thing we are going to do is to toss our bubbles to each other and move down the line," Olga stated in a matter of fact tone.

This was so cool for Billy. They all took turns throwing the bubbles to each other. It was lots of fun.

"Ok, class, next we are going to move onto our meditation mats," Olga explained. She provided mats on the floor with pillows. They were all in a circle with their heads pointing in and their feet pointing out. They formed into groups of eight. The door opened and several more large octopuses filed in purposefully.

Each one joined a group and sat in the middle. "This is for healing," Olga explained. "We are going to take three normal breaths, then one dolphin breath, and repeat this three times. When you take your last breath, you will receive an energy infusion from the dolphins. You will hold the sacred Merkaba, and your cells will be healed."

Billy was not sure what a Merkaba was, and why did he need one anyway? He tried to go along, but it nagged at Billy enough that he raised his hand and asked loudly, "What is a Merkaba anyway?"

Olga stopped and looked at him. "A Merkaba is a big blue star that surrounds everyone. If you look at it, the top of the star is about six inches above your head, and the bottom of the star is about six inches below your feet."

When Billy looked around, every person in the room had a big blue star surrounding him. It was clear and sparkled. It spun faster and faster. It looked like a space ship was around each of them and was too fast to see except for the color blue.

Billy closed his eyes and started to count. After the 12th breath, he did not remember anything until 30 minutes later. When he thought nothing was happening, he tried to move his fingers up off the floor. He was unable to. "So, ok," he thought, "something must be going on pretty big."

He could hear sniffles coming from other people. Olga said in her gentlest voice, "Start wiggling your fingers and toes, and when you are ready, move your legs and arms and slowly sit up. Take your time and breathe deeply." The adults seemed to have a much harder time, but everyone slowly rose from the floor and quietly filed out of the room. There was water, and most took a bottle with them. He grabbed a bottle and ran out the door with Sandy. Bubbles and Spinner met them at the door. It was time for their return trip.

Chapter 11

Healing of the Golden Rays

The next thing Billy knew, he was rubbing his eyes in his bed and sitting up. He remembered every part of the dream and swiftly wrote notes on the important parts so that he would not forget. He had all four pupples in the bed with him! Izzy said, "Welcome back," and Bella said, "We missed you."

Together they licked his face in glee. One on one side and one on the other! He could hardly write for laughing. Abbi was sitting at the bottom of the bed doing her tee-tee dance awaiting his attention. Tinker stretched slowly and licked his toes. She ambled up to his tummy and showed him she wanted her ears scratched as she would normally do every morning in greeting Billy.

His adventure had taken all night! He was surprised at the light coming in from the window. It felt like he was brand new! He giggled as he remembered all the amazing things that had occurred during the night.

Billy quickly got up and wrote everything down that he could remember and got dressed into his favorite bathing suit.

He ran down the stairs with the pupples following him! "Wait," they cried, "you have to tell us all about it!"

Izzy was trying to block him, and Bella was hanging on his heals! They were running around so quickly that Bella was running under Tink, and Izzy was jumping over her. Billy stopped for a moment and scratched all their ears and told them he would certainly do that when he had time, but he felt the need to get to the beach as quickly as possible for the next adventure. He knew it was coming, and it was as if someone was calling him from the beach!

"Wait for breakfast," said his Mom as he was coming down the stairs. When he saw his mom, he stopped and stared. She looked more like a mermaid than ever. She had another T-shirt on that said, "Why do they call it earth when it is mostly ocean?" It had two dolphins on it in the shape of a heart surrounding the words. "Like your T-shirt, Mom," Billy told her.

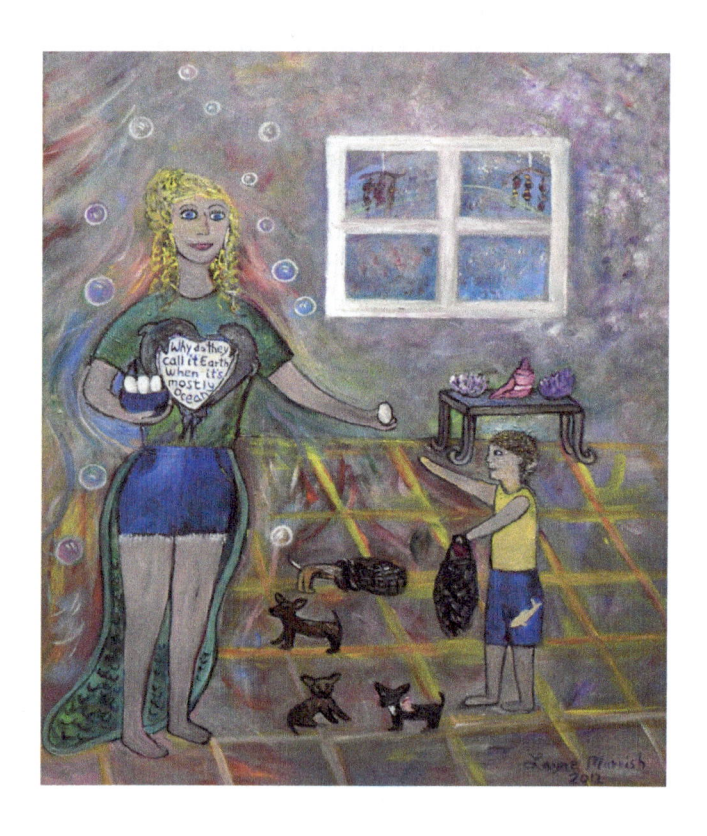

"Yep, I think I have a new favorite!" She said laughing. She looked at him closely. "Are you alright?" she asked.

"Yep, Mom! I had the best dream ever of mermaids and dolphins, and you were there!" said Billy excitedly.

"Cool!" She returned, "Can you tell me about it?"

"No time, Mom." He said dashing toward the door, "Got to get to the beach."

Billy's mom laughed out loud in her mermaid voice saying, "Well, let me know what you want to eat for breakfast!"

She gave him a boiled egg to eat on the way, and he hurried out the door to the beach.

The sun was shining again, and the beach sparkled like diamonds. No wind again, and as he looked at the emerald water, there were dolphins everywhere but they were not very close to shore. In the shallow water, there were many turtles. Billy was greeted by David the turtle, very briefly. "Just came by to check on you," said David. "You look great! Are you ready for your next adventure?" Just then Billy noticed many golden shapes swimming through the water. As he ventured closer, he noticed they seemed to be waving at him by putting their fins above the water and swimming along with him. He wandered closer to get a better look. A huge Golden Ray came right up to the shoreline where he was in just inches of water!

"What are you doing?" Billy asked.

"I just wanted to introduce myself," said the Ray.

"What is your name?" asked Billy.

"Raphael," said the Ray.

"Cool!" thought Billy. "I can talk to all kinds of beings."

"We need your help, Billy!" said the Golden Ray in a very low voice.

"What can I do for you?" asked Billy. He was using the dolphin rules and trying not to get too excited and just listen.

The Golden Ray explained, "We have a very important job in the ocean. It was given to us by the angel Raphael. It is to hold and absorb the negative vibrations from the earth and change them into love, but there is so much going on that is negative. We are being overwhelmed, and we need you to tell the angels to please help us to clear energies quicker. We need help!"

Billy lamented, "I don't know how!"

Raphael said, "Tell Bubbles to take our dilemma to the Cetacean National Conference, and they will know what to do. We are jumping out of the water to get some relief!"

Billy told him that he would gladly pass the message on and wandered further down the beach. He was sending golden rays of light into the water with each step he took to help the Golden Rays to heal themselves.

Suddenly he had an idea! The beaches were crystal! There were crystals in the radios! He could use the crystals as an antenna to call the angels and get the messages to them. He sat quietly with his hands in the sand and his heart wide open and called the angels. When he opened his eyes, the beach was full of balls of light and they were excitedly bouncing all around him. He spoke to the light balls out loud and a huge glowing golden angel appeared before him! He passed on the message to the angel from the Golden Rays, and the angel nodded his head and told him he would take care of it.

"Wait!" cried Billy, "What is your name?" The angel stood taller and said, "I am Raphael." His hair was golden yellow and his robe looked like spun gold with a braided belt loosely around his waist.

"How can you be named Raphael and the Golden Ray is named Raphael?" Billy asked.

"That is really very simple," said the angel. "In the higher vibrations, I am an angel and messenger. In the ocean, I am represented by many Golden Rays. I can be unlimited and both. The Golden Rays carry my vibration of love and healing to the earth via the seas. Golden Rays are many and the Golden Rays are one. Understand?" The angel asked.

"Not really," said Billy. He was a bit confused for it was quite mind-boggling.

"Someday you will understand very clearly," said the angel, softly.

"Ok," said Billy, "I will trust that."

In Raphael's hands, he had a golden scepter in one and a golden book in the other. Billy was in awe, but he thanked Raphael. When he looked at the water, there were Golden Rays covering the water and waving at them. They flew through the air and danced and played in the water. The very air and water was golden! It did not seem to be from the sun. As the angel slowly faded after going to the edge of the water and bowing to the Golden Rays, he and the colors gradually faded from Billy's sight.

Chapter 12
Billy and Sandy

Billy got up, brushed the sand off his suit and walked on down the beach looking for shells and enjoying the day!

Sandy came up behind him. She had a pink sun suit on and said quietly and shyly, "Hello. Remember me?"

Billy gave her a quick hug and said, "Of course, I do!" He studied her closely.

"Your name is Billy, and we met last night in school," she said quietly.

"You remember?" Billy asked in astonishment since he thought it was his dream adventure only. At that moment, he realized it had not been a dream at all.

"Of course I do," She said.

"Do you remember how to make the bubbles?" He asked.

They put their hands up at the same time and formed bubbles of energy. His was blue as the ocean and hers was pink with red swirls. They practiced cutting the bubbles in half and throwing them at each other for a few moments.

"Cool!" Billy said. "It really happened!"

"Yes, it did!" said Sandy.

They wandered along the beach for a moment in silence. They were deep in their own thoughts.

Then Sandy interrupted the silence. "Almera told me last night that if we wanted to, we could go with her and Solera and see their planets."

"How do we do that?" asked Billy.

"We simply ask, and they will take us," said Sandy.

Sandy and Billy played on the beach for several hours, picking up seashells, digging holes, talking about their night and what it meant, and how they could use the bubbles to play with and to help themselves. Billy told Sandy all about the pupples and how he was sure his mom was a magical mermaid. Sandy told Billy all about what it was like in her home and how careful she had to be. Her dad was very unhappy with the move that they had to make for his job and that Sandy's mother was working all the time, too. Sandy was very glad to have a friend to have adventures with and talk to.

The sun was warm and the day was moving very fast when they spotted the dolphins coming in. A pod of about 25 dolphins were gathering off the beach. Then they all did something very strange. They all came up at one time and looked toward the sky! They were in a circle and squeaking and squealing very loudly. Billy and Sandy started to walk toward them and go into the ocean to see what it was all about. They felt the presence of the whales, and the Golden Rays were swimming all around the dolphins.

"Look!" said Sandy, "They are here!"

A very large ship appeared in the sky. It was transparent and pink to begin with. "An Unidentified Flying Object!" cried Billy. "Look!"

Sandy said, "It is not a UFO if you know what it is! It is the ship that Almera, Neema and Solara come in! I have seen it before. It starts out very light pink and transparent and then gets more and more solid. After it gets solid, then usually Neema and Solara show up! I can't wait to see them!"

When Billy looked around, the beach was completely empty except for him, Sandy and the beings of the ocean. The dolphins all had their heads out of the water in a circle and were very still looking up at the pink ship that appeared very solid yet mysteriously translucent.

All at once there was a ringing sound from all the shells on the beach! Billy picked up one and held it to his ear like he has done a million times to hear the roar of the ocean, only this time it was different. He heard a voice coming from the shell!

"Billy is it alright for us to land?" asked a female voice.

"Who is this?" asked Billy in amazement.

"It is Neema," said the watery voice.

"What do you need to land?" asked Billy.

"We just did not want to scare you, so we wanted to call you on the shell phone and let you know we are landing," affirmed Neema.

"Yes," said Billy, "you can land." Billy looked at the shell and turned it over and over. He had never seen a shell do this before!

When the big blimp-like ship landed, a door opened and down the steps came Neema and Solara.

Neema had changed into a greenish blue flowing gown and Solara had a bright yellow vest and pants on. They walked down the stairs arm in arm. Billy was so surprised he had to sit down. It was broad daylight, and he did not understand where all the other people on the beach had gone. Then he looked around again. He saw the people were there, it just looked like they were under water, and moving very slowly. They did not seem to see the ship, Sandy or him. The only ones he could see clearly were the dolphins, Sandy, himself and Neema and Solara.

"How did you do that?" he asked Neema.

"We just shifted time a bit, and we are able to do all kinds of things to escape the notice of most people! Even if we just showed up, most people would not see us, because they are not paying attention. We are so far out of how most people think the world should be that even if we are seen, people put us out of their minds, but we have been visiting some people for years, just like we have been visiting Sandy. You and Sandy are very special to us and we always keep an eye on you!" explained Neema.

Billy thought about this for a while. He had a million questions but could get none of them out at the moment, he was so astonished.

"Don't worry Billy, we will answer all your questions as we go along, and you will see us again if you like. We have been waiting to meet you for years. Even though you feel you are different – and you are – this is the gift you have been given for this planet, and it will unfold as you grow up. Would you like to go for a ride in the ship? We have things to show you. So pick up the shell phone and contact your mom. Ask her if it is alright for you to come with us. I think she would like to come along," said Solara.

Billy picked up the shell and examined it all over for numbers to call his mom with. This was no simple cell phone.

"Ok! I give up. How do I call her?" Billy asked.

"Just speak her name and hold her picture in your mind, and she will answer. She has been using shell phones for years," said Neema.

"Mom?" said Billy into the shell phone.

In the kitchen, a very special shell Billy's mom kept on the window sill rang in a tinkling, watery way!

Billy's mom was in the living room when she heard it and ran to answer it. It did not ring often, but when it did, it was very important and must be answered right away!

"Hello?" Billy heard from the shell.

"Mom?" said Billy.

"Hi Billy, what do you need? I see you figured out our shell phone system!" she said with a laugh.

"Neema and Solaris are here and want to know if I can go for a ride with Sandy in a big pink spaceship," Billy pleaded. Billy really thought his mom would think he was just playing around. His Mom's answer shocked him.

"I will be right down, and we can all go. I love to ride in them!"

"Okay!" said Billy. He turned and asked Neema, "Now, how do I hang up?"

Neema laughed and said "Just put the shell back on the beach."

Billy carefully placed the shell back on the beach and stood and looked at it like he had never seen one before in his life. He then picked it back up and put it in his pocket.

"You can use it anytime you want to. You can call Bubbles, David, Humphrey or anyone you choose, anytime you choose by using this system," Neema explained. "Even us! And it can be any shell. When you pick up shells on the beach and hear the roar of the ocean, it is like a dial tone."

"Oh," crooned Billy, "I never knew!"

The tone of the shell also holds frequen-seas that will tune you into the ocean energies instantly.

"Wow!" exclaimed Billy. "I never knew! This is so cool!"

About that time, Billy's Mom walked up. She gave Neema and Solara a huge hug. Solara gave out a rumbling purr of happiness. Billy thought Solara still looked like a golden lion.

"I did not take the time to change for the trip," giggled Billy's mom. She still had a T-shirt with the message 'We are having a whale of a time!' printed on it with a big whale jumping out of the water. It had lots of old paint on it, and she had paint on her face and shorts. Her blond hair curled every which way.

"Well, what are we are waiting on?" she said. "Let's go!" Neema walked arm in arm with Billy's mom, and Sandy ran up the stairs with Solaris by her side. Billy was a bit slower. He was excited and a bit scared at the same time. Then he saw Bubbles peaking around the doorway. He ran up to her and asked, "How are you swimming on land and in the air?"

Bubbles gave a dolphin giggle! "We dolphins, whales and mermaids are very magical. We are masters at multidimensional travel. We call in the energy of the ocean and we can go anywhere. It's the same way you breathed under the water. It is magic! Come see."

Chapter 13

Earth's Future

The door to the large craft swooshed shut, and the ship started to move. Billy looked around the ship as they were going up. The walls were smooth and gray, and it looked like an airplane cabin that he had once gone into when flying to his grandma's except it was much simpler. The screens were all touch-activated and looked like large televisions for windows, but could be seen through easily. They all blinked on and off as they needed. There seemed to be no steering wheel like in the car, and he asked about that.

"We just think of where we need to go, and we are there," answered Solaris.

"It is time/quantum travel. We can go anywhere in the blink of an eye and at the speed of thought. Time and space are not in a straight line, and your scientists have much to learn about light, sound and travel," Solaris continued. "Time and space are really just loops and figure eights. We mastered this long ago."

Billy and Sandy ran to the window to look out at where they were going. They saw the earth from a distance. Many things surprised them. They had both seen many globes in school and had a pretty good idea of what the earth looked like from space from looking at it over the Internet.

It did not look the same.

"What is going on?" Billy asked with alarm.

There were many areas where the water of the oceans was a funny color, like an unhealthy yellow green or red, and there were many areas of the earth where the land was brown not green. The ice on the north and south poles was not as large as the globes showed, and there were many areas of the air that looked dirty.

"The earth is feeling the stress of humans not taking care of her," reported Neema sadly.

"What can we do?" cried Billy.

"Watch this," said Neema. "Do you remember your bubble? Just like you, the earth has energy around her, and we can shift it. Each human is very important in sending love and healing to the earth, just like each other." They all formed a circle around the ship and started sending love to the earth and bubbles of joy like a big circle of light and love beaming toward earth. Billy could see the beam coming from the ship. As he watched, a big blue beam went from the ship to the blue diamond mountain in Arkansas and made a connection, then he saw a grid of light start to form around the earth! It was just like the star that he had seen in Olga's class. A Merkaba she had called it. A huge blue star surrounding the planet! As it went around the earth, the water and air both changed colors and cleared up. On one television screen, he could see many people going to the beaches and sending this beautiful green and blue energy through all the crystals in the sand that connected up to the light grid and went all around the world. He realized Seasea was gathering up many people all over the world to do this every month. It was like soft fluffy clouds of energy coming from each person and transforming the water and air.

Neema shared with them, "We will show you that when each person sends love and healing to the earth, this is what happens. There are many of us doing this work to re-balance the earth and make it a better place, so we hope everyone will do this as often as possible. It does take a little longer for the earth and trees to heal than it does the air and water, but we have high hopes that there are enough people doing this healing work for the earth that all will be well. Let us show you another map." On this map were a few lights scattered all over the globe. Most were dim.

"This is how the lights of the people looked a few years ago. Not much enlightenment there for themselves or the planet. This was 50 years ago," Neema said. "Now we will show you every 10 years how it has changed."

With each picture, there were more and more people shining like beacons on the earth! Billy thought it was amazing. The last picture had a light on about every ten miles all over the earth. The earth looked like a sparkly lighted up Christmas tree.

"Humanity is changing as we speak!" exclaimed Neema. "There are many brave souls walking the earth simply holding the light now for the changes that are to come. Humans think they are just living their lives, and they are. But, at the same time, they are being a frequency of light upon the earth. It is the reason that you feel so different. It is because you are. Human DNA is changing, and you are a part of this change. It is not only important, it is vital to the earth. Before you were born, you agreed to do this. Many people do not understand how the children are changing. The children are creating how the planet will look in the future. It is bright and shining. The earth will turn into a star of love! It is a shining example for all the beings of the universes of how a planet can transform from fear to love and a blue shining star in one generation. That is why so many people from many other planets are watching Earth. So our message is to celebrate your differences and greet each other with love and respect and watch the earth transform!"

"It is beautiful!" Neema had tears of joy in her eyes as she spoke.

"There is so much light and love spreading across the planet. We did not think that humanity could change their hearts and light up the world in sparkles of joy and love, but humanity is really evolving into a race of light beings, just like us. We are so proud."

Bubbles was doing the tail slapping happy dance all around the cabin as Neema was talking.

"And we helped!" she said excitedly.

"Of course, all the dolphins helped. You are our Sea Stars!" said Neema.

"Well, I think we need to go home now," said Billy's Mom.

"Okay," said Neema, "Just close your eyes, and take a breath."

When Billy opened his eyes, the door to the ship was opening on the beach! They all walked onto the sand holding hands. Neema and Solara gave them each a big hug. They told them they would be back soon. Billy saw Bubbles and the other dolphins swimming away when he looked toward the gulf.

The door closed once more, and the ship grew more and more transparent until it went poof! and totally disappeared. Billy, Sandy and his mom looked at each other and suddenly all the other people on the beach were laughing, talking and moving at their normal speed. As it was time to go home, the three of them walked, squeaking their feet in the sand. Sandy gave Billy's mom a big hug and a hand squeeze and went to her home. Billy ran into the house and to write down his adventures on the computer so that this story could be told to everyone!

Appendix A
Bubble Exercise

Bubble Exercise can be found demonstrated in my youtube account under bubbles, or as it is printed here in its entirety.

Create a "Bubble of Energy" by putting your hands out and stating out loud:

Bubble of (Your Name) activate. If you do not feel the energy, then just pretend that it is there. If you visualize energy, see it forming. If you hear energy, hear it activating.

You will be working with statements in this bubble. Your job is to just observe your bubble as you work with these statements.

When you feel this bubble is fully activated, then either step into it or bring it over you. Now you are ready to start the process.

Say out loud:

I am (your name), All energies that are not my own, please leave my bubble now.

Breathe slow deep breaths several times. You may need to say this statement several times. Any emotions that come up, just breathe through them as you observe them. Allow the energies to leave your bubble without judgment. When you feel this step is complete, go to the next step.

Say out loud:

I ask all my Energy and Power, please return to me now. Take several deep breaths. Say this statement several times and breath. When you feel all your energies are returned, go to the next step.

Say out loud:

I ask my Highest Guides, Masters and Angels to join with me now. (along with any other people you would like to have there.) Take the time to notice and observe any differences you may feel.

Congratulate yourself on a job well done. This can be done anytime, anywhere, and just takes a moment. When you have it down, throw the circle away. You are a Master of this technique.

Optional statements:

Next statement is In This Moment, I am safe. Breathe through what ever comes up.

Optional: I love (your name). Breathe through what ever comes up.

When you are complete, know you carry your beautiful energy every where you go. When your bubble is clear, you are clear. Now add Joy to it! Add Love to it! Play with this and make it your own!

A couple of last thoughts: Remember! What you resist, persists. Energy is just that - Energy. When you observe and breathe through energy it automatically shifts and changes. Now go have fun!

Appendix B
Dolphin Rules for Shark Pools

One of the reasons that dolphins have such a need to help humanity is that humans at times make really bad decisions that hurt themselves, each other and worse, the very planet they live on. When I asked the dolphins what they wanted me to teach, they brought many situations into my life that showed me the areas that needed to be addressed. Remember also that sharks are at times our best friends and teachers.

All communications between dolphin pod mates will be from love and from the heart. If you are simply venting, please let the other pod mate know and go from there. The communications should be only about your own feelings about something or someone. The goal is to clear what ever button was pinged within yourself. Remember: It is all about your reactions and the gift each challenge brings to your life. Afterward, please protect the other person's privacy and let it go! All emotions are allowed when used to clear energies of your own. Emotions and communications will not be allowed if the intent is to judge, hurt or justify a position. Please keep all personal communication private unless given permission to share it.

None of us is perfect, and mistakes are allowed. If we are in higher vibrations and in a loving space, we can gently inquire as to the person's motives or where he was at. Never assume that you know what another person is thinking, feeling or experiencing. You are probably wrong. Dolphins shift very quickly and easily and effortlessly. Ask before assuming. As best you can, always be as clear and truthful in your communications with others.

If something is causing an angry, hurtful, unloving response within you, please wait before any engagement with the perceived cause (person), because perhaps it is time to have a discussion with your ego. Say out loud "I love you, Ego, and I ask you to step aside so that I can hear what spirit needs to tell me or receive what ever lesson there is in this situation." You may have to repeat this a couple of times depending on how much reassurance your ego needs in this moment. Dolphins create safe space for everyone including themselves.

You will find it easier and more comfortable for both of you to communicate from your heart space. Whether e-mail, phone call or sitting down to discuss it with the intent to take responsibility and get clear in a positive way, never write an e-mail to the pod or each other that comes from anger, hurt or justification for bad or inappropriate behavior. Write each e-mail in a way that you would not mind the person who you are speaking of reading it. Dolphins bring everything to the surface and seek clarity, truth and light. Believe me, if you write or speak something about someone that you do not want him to read, he probably will. E-mails are not private. Once you write something, you can't take it back. Dolphins do not purposely damage or hurt any member of their pods.

If you have someone who you can't reach resolution with, swim away. Go do something else. Dolphins have a higher purpose, and keep it in mind at all times. If you are stuck in a stagnant pool, play while you wait for the tide to come up. It always will. Send lots of Bubbles of Love and Light to that person or situation and to yourself. Spirit will handle it, and it might not be for or about you, even when it is pinging your buttons.

Ask yourself "Do I want to be right or do I want to be happy?" Sometimes you just have to let it go and play and move. Play shifts energy. Emotions, once fully accepted and loved, always shift. We can swim in higher clearer waters, but we have to choose to do so as we are ready.

Allow yourself and others to have their own experiences without judgment. Dolphins are masters at observation while remaining in connection with their hearts. It is not an easy thing for humans. It takes real commitment, practice and patience, but with practice it becomes easier. Play with it.

You will not reach agreement on everything in the human world. At times, you just have to agree to disagree. Honor each person's beliefs, even if you do not agree with them. It is a key to humanity's future.

Take the time to nurture yourself. You matter, and loving yourself is key. Dolphins are very secure in who they are and what they are about. Humanity? Not so much. If you are not sure how you feel about something, simply sit with the question. The answer will flow to you.

A rule in quantum physics is energy observed is in constant motion. Reach for the higher shifts in energy. Lower energy is chaos, confusion and dark. Higher energy's are clear, smooth and light. Observation while made in the Joy and Love vibrations automatically shifts all the energies higher. Remember that.

The deeper you dive, the higher you can jump. The more you go within and clear, the more you can bring to the world. When you have a clearer space within yourself, you have more room in your heart for joy, love, abundance and peace. The more you can hold the higher vibrations and frequencies, the better you will feel on every level. This takes time, effort and real commitment to yourself. Your journey is your responsibility. This means you assess where you are, and have at least an idea of where you see yourself in the future. We can all strive to be better Dolphins. Not perfect, just better. Dolphins encourage total submersion and connection within yourself and flying high to take your beautiful frequencies into the world. Be a good example of a Dolphin walking the earth.

No means no. Dolphins only engage when they want to and are ready to. Then they are fully engaged and present. If someone is not ready for engagement, then honor that. If you have an agenda, have a need or want in a situation, state it clearly and up front. Be very clear in your communications with each other. If someone is not clear, stop and explore this until you both are. This will take time, energy and real commitment to yourself and to the other person. Allow plenty of time and understand that it is really about being heard and accepted.

Keep your word and maintain integrity at all times. If you are unable to keep your word, contact the person and let him know as soon as possible. You can then reach a different agreement. It is a very important part of building safe space and trust. Dolphins are all about maintaining fluidity and flow. But everyone needs to be clear in the direction that he is going in. If it changes, please let others know as quickly as possible.

We do not own any Frequency or Vibration, but we do own how we present it to the world. While we are all connected on many levels, we each have gifts to bring to the world in creative and unique ways. When we are in the love and joy frequencies, we all have the ability to swim into an ocean of knowledge and receive gifts from spirit. Many times I have called others and received the same message from spirit as someone else. I have always been excited and pleased about this synchronization and called it confirmation of my messages, and many times I do not share information that I have received until I do get confirmation. Not everyone feels the same way. I honor that also.

So I ask, as you embody the dolphin, ocean and spirit messages and take them out into the world, I encourage you to make them your own. Feel free to discuss any and all ideas on how to create these teachings in a better way. I am open to all suggestions and excited about new ideas! Please do not share copy written material, unless you copy it exactly along with the credits.

Please do not use the exercises exactly as presented. Use your very best and honorable judgment in taking full credit with these teachings and what you have learned. I ask you not to teach what you have learned until you and spirit agree on a certain level of Mastery. You will know beyond a doubt when you are ready as spirit and the dolphins will clearly show you where to go and what to do. It will be easy and flow to you.

The credit really goes to the dolphins and the wise beings of the sea, along with angels and all Beings on High who are teaching and striving for a better Humanity. I am grateful for their wisdom and teachings. I am grateful for each of their lessons for Humanity and how to live on this beautiful planet with love, wisdom and grace. I have borrowed from many sources and ideas.

You take the gifts that you can use from this book, and if you are not in alignment with any of the teachings, please put them to the side for now. They may come in handy later as we all learn and grow.

Always remember, Ego says Mine, Spirit says Ours. Choose your position wisely.

I would like to share one more thought for the day that came to me clearly in conversation with a dear friend.

When we are operating from "ego", we are humans having a spiritual experience. When we are in our hearts, we are spirits having a human adventure. Have your adventures with JOY!

Biography

Cyndie Lepori graduated from the University of Southern Mississippi with a Bachelor of Science Degree. Her Major was nursing with a minor in Psychology. She gives credit for this background in nursing for her becoming a medical intuitive working on Quantum Levels.

As a Level 13 Ascension Reiki Master Teacher since 1994, she has taught over 350 students in Mississippi and around the world. She has also taught Reiki Groups in Mississippi for seven years. Cindy has been a guest lecturer at the University of Southern Mississippi and at Milsaps College on Alternative Therapies, and has been a speaker at many workshops, festivals, and conventions.

Cyndie is a certified Lifesprings Graduate. This training included the Leadership and Masters programs. She is certified by Linda Shay of Dolphin Healing HeArt World as a Dolphin Energy Practitioner/Healer Level II. Having traveled the world, she has spread the light to Mexico, Spain, California, Hawaii, Cayman Islands, Bahamas, and Holland.

Cyndie is a Dolphin, Whale and Animal Communicator. As a sailor and PADI scuba instructor, she has a deep and abiding relationship with the ocean, dolphins and whales. As a clear channel, she has earned the Mantle of Authority to remove and heal Karmic Records and Patterns as well as assist in healing negative energies and entities. This incorporates her ability as a transition specialist in service to people or animals who have transitioned, assisting them into areas for further education and healing by the angels until they are ready for the light. She works directly with the Angels and Masters in service to the Earth and to Humanity.

Cyndie clears properties and resets energies with the placement of vortexes and positive energies in homes or on properties. She has been creating events for the healing of the world for several years by establishing energetic connections with the grid and the crystalline beaches in Florida. These events have tied in people from all over the planet who have joined in during these beach activations.

Cyndie presents Bubbles of Joy Week-ends, Dolphin Playshops and is a guest speaker at events and festivals, including dolphin trips. As an intuitive healer, and reader she offers private sessions. Readers can contact her directly for further information or check out her website for updates on coming events.

Cyndie says she wrote this book to assist children and grownups who want to better understand the gifts of spirit the dolphins have provided for us. She believes that we are all gifted, yet because of the challenges we face as humans those gifts for many have become lost. Her desire for those who read this book, both young and old, is for them to reacquaint and connect themselves with their own special gifts. More importantly she wants the reader to establish a heart to heart connection with themselves, one another and then the world. Heart to heart connections and unity for humanity are the true gifts of the dolphins. She says, "Eye to eye and heart to heart, we will create a better future."

Cyndie Lepori

Photographer: Courtland William Richards

Contact Information:

Author:

Cyndie Lepori

182 County Road 533-7

Stringer MS 39481

601.466.6559

www.dolphinhugs4u2.com

dolphinhugs4u2@aol.com

Dolphinhugs4u2@gmail.com

http://www.facebook.com/#!/cyndie.lepori

http://www.dolphinhugs4u2.com/cyndie (newsletter)

Illustrator:

Layne Keeton Murrish

P.O. Box 709

Redway CA 95560

707-923-1660

www.thepeacefulpainter.com

peacefullpainter@gmail.com

http://www.facebook.com/#!/layne.keeton.murrish

Bubbles and Billy Sandwalker

When Billy meets a dolphin named Bubbles, he begins to see his life, the lives of the dolphins and other colorful characters in a new and wonderful way. These adventures profoundly change not only how he thinks of himself and his place in this world, but how he views the others in the story as well.

It is a wonderfully positive inspiring adventure story full of mermaids, dolphins, and ETs, that will keep you turning every page, reading it many times and sharing with others. This beautifully written and illustrated story is not just a book for children, but a book for all ages and will be read over and over for years to come.

If you enjoyed Johnathan Livingston Seagull, you will love this book too. You will never see dolphins, pupples, or others in the same way again.